This igloo book belongs to:

....

igloobooks

Original story by Lewis Carroll
Retold by Jan Payne
Illustrated by Eva Morales

Cover designed by Lee Italiano
Interiors designed by Justine Ablett
Edited by Hannah Cather

Copyright © 2017 Igloo Books Ltd

An imprint of Igloo Books Group,
a Bonnier Publishing company
www.bonnierpublishing.com

Published in 2018
by Igloo Books Ltd, Cottage Farm
Sywell, NN6 0BJ
All rights reserved, including the right of reproduction
in whole or in part in any form.

Manufactured in China. GUA009 0518
10 9 8 7 6 5 4 3 2

Library of Congress Cataloging-in-Publication
Data is available upon request.

ISBN 978-1-4998-8004-5
IglooBooks.com
www.bonnierpublishing.com

Alice in Wonderland

igloobooks

One sunny afternoon, Alice and her sister were sitting in the garden. Her sister had her nose in a book and Alice was bored. She was just about to begin making a daisy chain when a white rabbit, with pink eyes, ran past. **"I'm late! I'm late!"** cried the White Rabbit.

The White Rabbit scurried off across the lawn. **"Oh my ears and whiskers!"** he cried, diving down a round, dark hole.

"Wait for me," called Alice, running after him.

She peered down the hole and, before she knew it, Alice felt herself **falling**. Down, down she went.

Alice landed, **bump**, on a pile of leaves. Ahead, she could just see the White Rabbit disappearing down a long passageway.

She followed him and found a tiny gold key lying on a glass table. The key opened a little door, beyond which was a beautiful garden.

"I'm too big to get through," said Alice.

Then, on the table, she saw a bottle with a label that said, **'drink me.'**

"Curiouser and curiouser," whispered Alice. She took a sip from the bottle.

drink me

Suddenly, she began to **shrink.** Soon, Alice was no bigger than the White Rabbit.

Alice went to open the door, but found she had left the key on the table.

She cried and cried and soon, Alice was floating in a pool of tears.

"Grab my tail," called a mouse as he swam toward her. The mouse towed Alice to a safe place on the shore.

After a while, Alice heard the pattering of footsteps as the White Rabbit ran up to her. **"My goodness! I'm late! Oh my fur and whiskers!"** Thinking Alice was his maid, he told her to go into his house and fetch his gloves and fan.

So Alice went inside the White Rabbit's house.

Inside the cottage, a table was set with scrumptious things to eat, including a chocolate cake with the words 'eat me' on it in icing. Alice cut a piece and took a large bite.

Suddenly, she felt herself getting taller and taller and taller, until, with a bump, her head hit the ceiling.

The White Rabbit was cross. **"I have an appointment with the Queen,"** he said, **"and you are blocking the door."**

Alice sobbed and, without thinking, fanned herself with the White Rabbit's magic fan. Immediately, she began to shrink. **"Will I ever be my right size again?"** she wailed.

Alice left the White Rabbit's house and walked on. Soon, she heard a sleepy voice, but saw no one, only a mushroom that was about her size. Stretching on tiptoe, Alice peered over the edge and saw a large blue caterpillar, smoking a strange pipe.

"Who are you?" it asked.

"I hardly know who I am," said Alice, "I change so often."

"If you eat two pieces of my special mushroom, one will make you bigger and one will make you smaller," said the Caterpillar.

So, Alice ate one piece of the mushroom and instantly began to grOW. Soon, she was her normal size again.

"I really must go and try to get into the garden," said Alice.

Soon, Alice came to a house where a duchess was sitting by a cat that grinned from ear to ear. **"Why does your cat grin like that?"** asked Alice.
"Because it's a Cheshire Cat," answered the Duchess. **"Now, I must go and play croquet with the Queen."** With that, she hurried away.

Outside, Alice was startled to find the Cheshire Cat grinning at her from a branch. "Cheshire Cat, which way should I go from here?" she asked.

"The March Hare's house is that way," said the Cat. "Do you play croquet with the Queen today?"

"I haven't been invited," replied Alice, but the Cat just smiled and slowly disappeared.

Alice followed the Cheshire Cat's directions until she came to a pretty garden, where the March Hare and the Hatter were having tea under a tree. Sitting on a teapot in front of them, fast asleep, was the Dormouse.

"No room!" they cried out, huddling together, when they saw Alice.

"**There's plenty of room,**" said Alice crossly, and sat down in a large armchair. "**How rude,**" she thought, as the March Hare dipped his watch in a teacup and the Hatter talked in riddles.

The Hatter opened his eyes wide and said, **"Why is a raven like a writing desk?"**
Alice thought and thought about ravens and writing desks.
"Have you guessed the answer yet?" asked the Hatter.
"No, I give up," Alice replied. **"What's the answer?"**
"I haven't the slightest idea," said the Hatter.

Alice was very confused indeed, so she got up and walked off. **"I'll never come here again,"** she said. **"This is the most absurd tea party I've ever been to."**

Alice left the garden and walked back to the woods, just as the Hatter and the March Hare were putting the Dormouse into the teapot.

In the woods, Alice found a door that led back to the glass table with the gold key. Nibbling the second piece of the Caterpillar's mushroom, Alice shrank. Soon, she was small enough to unlock the tiny door and enter the little garden.

There, she found pretty heart-shaped trees and brightly colored flowers.

Suddenly, a procession came toward Alice and there were shouts of, **"The Queen! The Queen!"** Alice saw the White Rabbit, the Knave of Hearts, and then the King and Queen of Hearts.

"Who are you?" asked the Queen.

"Alice, Your Majesty," replied the girl. **"You shall play croquet,"** commanded the Queen.

Alice thought she had never seen such a curious croquet ground in her life. The croquet balls were live hedgehogs and the mallets, live flamingos.

The card soldiers had to use their hands and feet to make the arches.

The players all played at once, without waiting for turns, quarreling all the while, and fighting for the hedgehogs.

In a very short time, the Queen was in a furious temper and went stamping about and shouting, **"Off with his head!"** about once a minute.

Alice was looking around for some way of escape,
when she noticed the Cheshire Cat had appeared.

"How are you doing?" asked the Cat.

"I don't think they play at all fairly,"
Alice said, in a rather complaining tone.
"They all quarrel and don't seem to
have any rules in particular."
"How do you like the Queen?"
asked the Cheshire Cat, in a whisper.
"Not at all," replied Alice, tucking her
flamingo mallet under her arm and
going off to find her hedgehog.

On the way, she met the Duchess and chatted happily with her until someone shouted . . .

. . . "The trial's started!"

In the courtroom, the King and Queen were seated on their thrones and the Knave of Hearts stood before them. The White Rabbit began to speak . . .

"The Queen of Hearts,
she made some tarts,
all on a summer's day.
The Knave of Hearts,
he stole those tarts
and took them quite away!"

"Call the witness!" cried the King. Suddenly, Alice had the curious feeling that she was beginning to **grOW**.

"Alice!" shouted the White Rabbit. Alice jumped up and ran over to the witness stand, tipping it over in the process.

"What do you know about this business?" the King said to Alice.

"Nothing whatsoever," replied Alice.

The King asked the jury to consider their verdict.
"No, no!" cried the Queen. **"Sentence first, verdict afterwards."**

By this time, Alice had grown **bigger**.

"Stuff and nonsense!"
she said loudly. **"The idea of having
the sentence before the verdict!"**

"Hold your tongue!"
shouted the Queen.

"I won't!" cried Alice.

"Off with her head!" screamed the Queen. By now, Alice was almost her full size. **"Who cares about you?"** she shouted. **"You're nothing but a pack of cards!"**

At this, the whole pack rose up and came flying down upon Alice. The cards were soon spinning all around her, so Alice closed her eyes and wished them away.

Suddenly, Alice found herself lying on a bank in the garden.
Her head was in the lap of her sister, who was gently brushing away
some dead leaves that had fluttered down from the trees upon her face.
"Wake up, Alice dear," said her sister. **"It's nearly time for tea."**

"Oh, I've had such a curious dream," said Alice.

She told her sister, as well as she could remember, all the strange and magical things that had happened in her adventure.

When she had finished, Alice got up and ran off, thinking what a wonderful dream it had been.

Discover three more enchanting classic tales. . . .

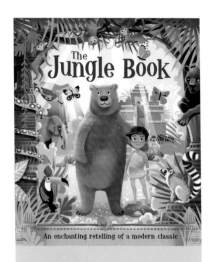

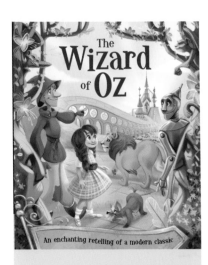

Join Mowgli as he learns the strange ways of the jungle, ever guided by the wise bear, Baloo. This retelling of the timeless classic, with beautiful illustrations, will capture every child's imagination.

Set sail on a rip-roaring adventure in this classic story of swashbuckling pirates and hidden treasure. This exciting tale, with stunning original illustrations, is perfect for a thrilling storytime.

Be swept away with Dorothy and Toto to the Land of Oz, where they meet a talking Scarecrow, Tin Man, and Lion. This retelling of the well-loved classic tale is sure to make storytime exciting.

Look out for these other exciting tales
in our storytime series!

igloobooks